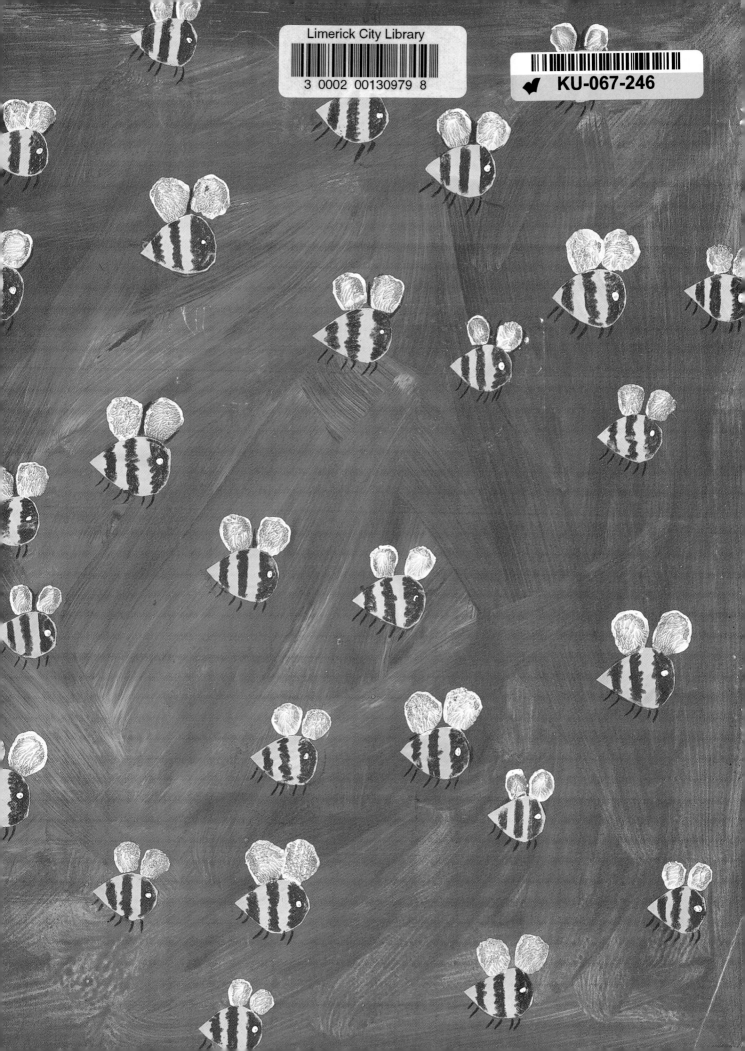

For Mum and Dad

Great Clarendon Street, Oxford OX2 6DP

Oxford   New York

Athens   Auckland   Bangkok   Bogota
Buenos Aires   Calcutta   Cape Town   Chennai
Dar es Salaam   Delhi   Florence   Hong Kong
Istanbul   Karachi   Kuala Lumpur   Madrid
Melbourne   Mexico City   Mumbai   Nairobi
Paris   Sao Paulo   Singapore
Taipei   Tokyo   Toronto   Warsaw

and associated companies in
Berlin   Ibadan

Oxford is a trade mark of Oxford University Press

© Joanne Partis 2000

First published 2000

10 9 8 7 6 5 4 3 2 1

Joanne Partis has asserted her moral right to be
known as the author of the work.

A CIP catalogue record for this book is available
from the British Library

ISBN 0 19 279048 X (hardback)
ISBN 0 19 272387 1 (paperback)

Printed in Hong Kong

Stripe

Joanne Partis

OXFORD

UNIVERSITY PRESS

Stripe lived with
his mum and dad on
the edge of a huge jungle.
'Never go there by yourself,' said his mum.
'It's very dangerous.'
One hot afternoon, his mum and dad fell asleep.

'The jungle looks very cool,' thought Stripe.
'Perhaps I'll go in there, just for a minute.'

Stripe trotted happily through the trees,
all the time getting further and further
away from home.

Just then, he spotted a bee's nest
high up in a tree.
'Honey,' thought Stripe, excitedly.

But as he stretched up to reach it,
he heard a loud buzzing noise.

The bees were
cross and chased
poor Stripe away . . .

. . . right out of the jungle . . .

. . . and into the river!

Under the water
Stripe was safe from
the bees.

Cautiously, he swam up to the surface
and pulled himself on to a log. The bees
had all gone – but Stripe had a feeling
that he was being watched.

The river was full of hungry crocodiles!
Stripe paddled hard as they chased
him down the river . . .

. . . and out to sea.
Just as the snapping jaws
were getting closer and closer,

Stripe spotted a cave in the distance.
It looked like a good place to hide.

But the closer he got, the stranger it looked.

It was not a cave at all, but a whale's mouth.

Inside the whale it was very cold and very dark.
Stripe was scared. Then he had an idea.

With the tip of his tail he tickled the top of the
whale's mouth . . .

ACHOOOO

The whale sneezed and Stripe flew high
up into the air.

And then he was . . .

falling . . .

falling . . .

falling ...

Bump!

Stripe landed back home, and there were
his mum and dad just waking up.

'I won't go back to
the jungle for a long,
long time,' thought Stripe.

And he curled up
and went to sleep.

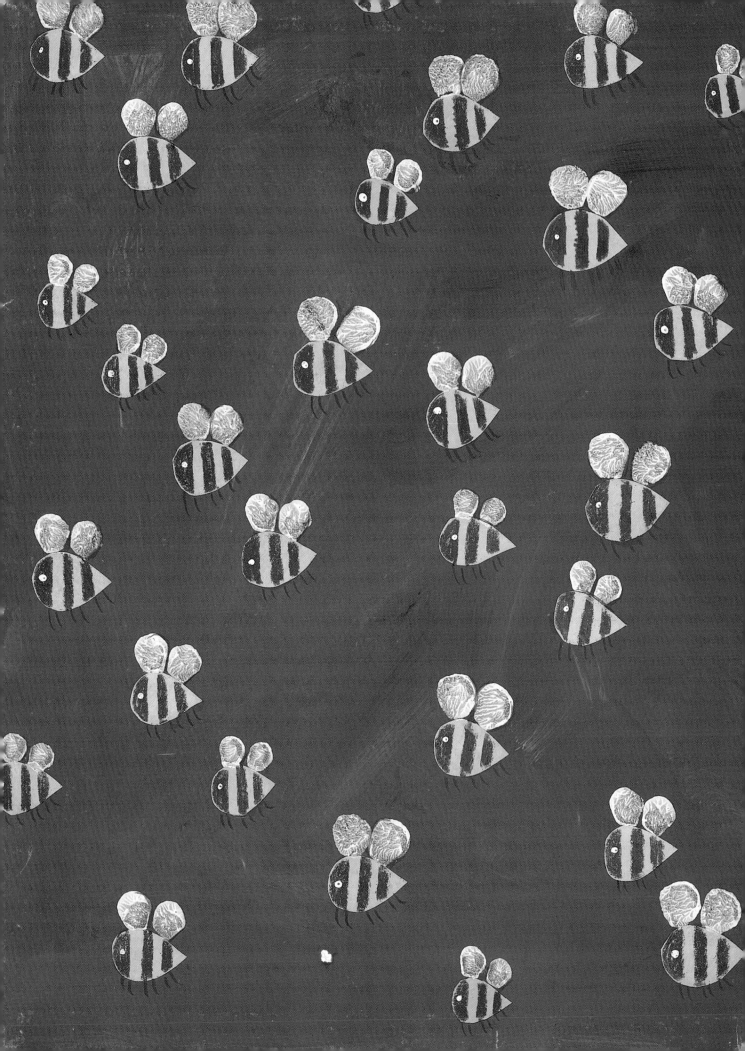